The Indian Girl's Definitive Guide to Staying Single

Nivi Engineer

Copyright © 2012 Nivi Engineer

All rights reserved.

ISBN:1478229039

ISBN-13: 978-1478229032

DEDICATION

To my sister, who inspired this story, and my brother-in-law, who ended her streak.

CONTENTS

	Acknowledgments	i
	Introduction	1
1	Don't Break Out In Bhangra	4
2	Sorry, Sari!	9
3	Don't Bolo the Bhasha / Hold Back the Hindi	16
4	Never Let Them See You Cook	20
5	Chase Away the Chai	25
6	Maro the Mind Games	33
7	Beware the Biodata	44
8	Sabotage the Shaadi Shot	52
9	Flaunt Facebook: Make Your Social Network Your Naukar	58
10	Make Masala of the Meet and Greet	64
11	Be You, Be True, Bindaas	76

ACKNOWLEDGMENTS

Maura O'Beirne-Stanko and my sister, Thank you for your insightful critiques and encouragement. To my brother for being so bindaas (and introducing me to the term).

INTRODUCTION

If you're reading this, then you have undoubtedly been asked by your parents and their friends, and probably by your friends, when you are planning on getting married. The nice thing is, in this day and age, we girls have a little longer to go before we're considered unmarriageable, but do keep in mind that this is thanks to your fellow Indian single sisters. We have been paving the way with our stubbornness and unwillingness to compromise our dreams in order to live by rules that simply don't allow for our freedom.

Now, I have nothing against marriage. I grew up watching the same Indian movies as everyone else. My friends would gaze dreamily at Akshay Kumar and Amir Khan, envying Karina Kapoor, Juhi Chawla, and the other actresses whose characters were lucky enough to find that special man who worked hard, cared for his family, was highly moral, and looked incredibly hot. Their heroes were willing to fight for their girls, and they always lived happily ever after.

I, meanwhile, rolled my eyes at how the girls, no matter how 'tough' they were, instantly gave in to his charms. I groaned when the girls learned that the key to a happily-ever-after involved giving up any career aspirations and choosing to stay home, raise children, and take care of the house. This typical Indian movie formula worked well for most parental audiences, since this was the life they wished their daughters to lead after graduation. But if the idea of this kind of future makes you cringe, then read on. This guide was written to help you avoid matrimony. Just keep in mind that by publishing this guide, there is always the potential that this may fall into the wrong hands. So protect it well, and always be on your guard.

Remember, you are on the market, whether you want to be or not, and you need to think carefully about what your choices are saying about you. Hopefully this guide will help you become more self-aware, so that the message you send is the one you wish to convey.

RULE #1
DON'T BREAK OUT IN BHANGRA

My parents moved here from India after they got married. My sister and I were born and raised here, but my parents were clearly set on raising us with Indian standards. They were so afraid of our losing our Indian culture that we were never allowed to go to school dances. They taught us to read and write Hindi, and we watched Indian movies every Friday and Saturday night. We socialized with other Indian families. I know I have criticized the movies, but as sheer entertainment, I confess I did enjoy them. My friends and I would watch the songs again and again, learning the dance steps. When we'd visit India, we'd return with plenty of great outfits that we'd wear to parties and when doing dances. First our moms choreographed dances that we would perform on stage at our local Indian community functions - for Holi in March, India's Independence Day on August 15, and Diwali in October. Soon, we chose our own songs and mimicked the dance steps we saw in the movies, ultimately choreographing the dances ourselves.

    One summer, an Indian dance instructor came to town. Over the course of four weeks, my sister, our friends, and I were dropped off at the high school gym every day and learned eight different dances. At the end of the month, we performed these dances in front of an audience of about one hundred Indians from the community. Together, these dances told a story - though I never did pay attention to what it was. I just had fun hanging out with my friends all day, and since I loved to dance, I had a blast doing that as well.

What I didn't realize was that our parents were pretty wily. We thought we were so smart, appeasing them by at least dancing to Indian songs, but drawing the line at taking lessons in one of the intense South Indian dance styles (we also had friends that learned Kathak and Bharatanatyam, and while we acknowledged that they were probably way more talented dancers than us, it just didn't seem fun to us). We would watch those girls getting ready in the dressing rooms backstage at the programs, and didn't envy all the time and detail it took. Sure, they looked beautiful, but my friends and I could get dressed quickly and run around the halls with the boys, only to get yelled at to return when we were needed backstage. I thought we had pulled off quite the scam - getting credit for doing the dance, but with much less effort than all the other girls. We could go on stage and show the world (or at least the Indian community) that we've got rhythm, talent (we did, after all, choreograph the dances ourselves), and a keen fashion sense. That and the fact that we weren't scared little wallflowers that couldn't handle the spotlight. I was proud of my dancing and didn't mind showing it.

What I didn't realize at the time is that from our mothers' point of view, by going on stage dressed in Indian clothes (that were always respectably modest), we were showing our beauty, a love of Indian culture and tradition, and our willingness to obey our parents (there were always kids who refused to dance, but that made us look so much more cultured, right?). After all, what are these dances but a way to showcase the fine marriageability of the community's daughters?

So, don't do it. Don't let yourself get drawn into the marriage market that way. Or, if you must dance, make sure you stick with group dances (the more people the better), never do solos during those dances, and never, ever, ever dance alone. Blend into the crowd. That's your best way to avoid being regarded too closely by the Indian dads and moms who are hoping to find a good Indian girl for their handsome and smart but shy son.

RULE #2
SORRY, SARI!

You know how I mentioned that I loved stocking up on the latest Indian fashions when we would go to India? Well, while the clothes are gorgeous, comfortable, and can flatter any figure, they also send a dangerous message if you're hoping to stay single. Depending on what kind of outfit you're wearing, you will say something different. But in all cases, the message is the same: I am marriageable.

Get all fancied up, go all out with the hair, makeup and accessories, and you are a catch! Those aunties will be thinking, "You would make a beautiful bride, and you are the only one beautiful enough for my magnificent son." And keep in mind that all mothers find their sons magnificent, even if he is 'going through a phase' with facial piercings and a mohawk. In that case, you would be just the kind of girl her son would need to straighten himself out (but not to the point of being submissive, since her son would be the head of the household).

What if you simplify the makeup and jewelry, but still look presentable enough that your mother won't drag you back to her room to add more? Well, what a sensible wife you will be. You are sure then to draw the attention of those Indian dads and moms of handsome and smart but shy sons. You are not some flighty girl who will spend so much time on your looks that you neglect your husband.

Okay then, how about simple, nondescript clothes, you ask? There's one of two things that could happen. Either the mother sees you as a project - clay that she can mold into a beautiful sculpture (so that her son looks better for having made you as beautiful as you can be), or she will see you as maid-worthy, someone who will work hard and be under her control. Definitely appealing qualities in a daughter-in-law, don't you think?

So what about the different outfits? Never wear saris. They look good on every Indian woman, and make you look grown up, which means that you look more like the daughter-in-law you could become. Don't make it so easy for them to imagine you as a good wife and bahu (daughter-in-law). As for lehengas - you know, the fitted bodice and long skirt with the matching shawl? You do know that's what brides wear on their wedding day, don't you? But, if you must, don't wear any shade of red unless you really do want to announce to everyone that you're looking for a husband.

That leaves the whole array of what I like to call kurtha wear. There's the top - and it tends to be longer (unlike the sari and lehenga blouses). It can be fitted or loose, go just to the waist or down past your knees. It can have many different necklines and come in varying degrees of fanciness. The pants can be churidars ('skinny leg'), salwars (wide-bottom), or the sharara (which has a shorter top and ornate pants that flare out at the feet). If you're trying to stay single, you'll want to stick with kurtha wear for as long as possible. It is, after all, what is worn by young girls in India on a daily basis. To be clear, I'm not saying you should wear Indian clothes every day; on the contrary, avoid it as much as you can or you'll send the message of being very culturally sensitive and again be far more appealing to potential mothers-in-law.

All these outfits can be quite flattering. That can be a bad thing, because while you don't want the Aunties and Uncles out there to see you as a purchaseable product, you also don't want to end up either a) being seen as too immodest that your reputation is tarnished, or b) drawing the attention of the Indian boy who will then also side with his parents on the potential arrangement of a union.

You might think you don't care about your reputation, because it could help you stay single. But there are two problems with that approach. One, what if you change your mind later about wanting to get married? You don't want to irreparably damage your chances. And two, it may not only be the parents of boys that think badly of you; your friends' parents may not wish you to tarnish their own daughters' reputations by associating with you. Worse, your friends may agree, and is one outfit really worth risking a friendship? You can really only decide for yourself, but that just seems like a lot of pressure to put on one outfit to make it worth the hassle.

There are a couple more options that do bear mentioning. Kurthis are Indian tops that 'go with anything'. They are sold by themselves, and can be worn with jeans, a nice skirt, or even slacks. You might be thinking that kurthis seem like the perfect solution, that they seem to be sufficiently Indian while still allowing you to say 'hey, I'm an American'. The problem is, you are telling your future in-laws that you are comfortable with your Indian side, you eat Indian food, and that you probably speak Hinglish (a mix of Hindi and English that demonstrates proficiency in both languages - even if you had intended it as a way to seem ignorant); in other words, their future grandchildren will still be Indian. Congratulations, you've just moved up the ranks.

Which leads us to Western clothes. Yes, this is by far the most effective way to stave off marriage, though the same risks occur as with other clothes. You don't want to come across as being ignorant of your Indian heritage, because that is hard to overcome. Wait too long to switch to Indian and it is seen as a desperate attempt to find a good husband. You don't want to be disrespectful - if you go to a puja, by all means, wear Indian clothes. Religious ceremonies often require you to cover your head at certain times, and you don't want to be messing up the look of your outfit by borrowing your mother's shawl and looking a total fool. Have some self-respect, girl. But to any other occasion, tasteful, classy Western clothes tell the world that you are respectable, well-groomed, and stylish, while being strong enough to stand your ground and be yourself. Any decent mother-in-law would be impressed with these qualities, since it would mean that your future children won't be spoiled. Darn, I forgot about that.

RULE #3
DON'T BOLO THE BHASHA / HOLD BACK THE HINDI

Now, I'm not saying that if your parents speak Hindi in the house that you should make no effort to learn it. That, after all, is key to preventing them from plotting about you right in front of your face. Oh no, ignorance is not an option. Since we were little, my parents would talk to each other at the dinner table in Hindi. Because of the names they threw around, we knew they were talking about our aunts and uncles in India, or about their friends. And they would throw in enough words in English that we could catch the general gist of the conversation. Then, after years of watching Indian movies, and being dragged to Hindi school by our mother, we actually learned the language.

It's useful to know the language, because you definitely need to be able to know what people are saying about you. Just remember, there are strict rules for the usage of this knowledge. First, never give yourself away. It is entirely possible to get through Hindi school with only a marginal knowledge of the language. Work hard to learn it, but don't let anyone know that you do. For example, you should never doodle Hindi words on anything that can be found (If, for example, you leave your math notebook sitting open on the kitchen table the evening before your midterm, only to have it discovered by your mother while you go to the bathroom, and if you happen to have written someone's name - or worse, your own name with a different last name - well, there's little help I can provide, regardless of the language in which the name was written).

As for learning Hindi, study under your covers late at night, if you must, but never in public. This is definitely harder to do if your mother is your teacher, but it is still possible. When you're at a party eavesdropping, don't get caught. No laughing at the jokes, no reacting to the information, and no discussing anything you heard until after you get home. And then, if you're discussing it on the phone with a friend, for goodness sake, have the good sense to go to your room and shut the door; you know full well that once your mother learns that you know Hindi, she will brag about it to all her friends, and your cover will be blown.

Over time, you may reveal some knowledge of Hindi, and consequently your parents will address you in Hindi. By no means should you ever respond in Hindi. Get them used to listening to English. You are doing them a favor, after all, helping them adapt to life in America (feel free to remind yourself of this fact if you struggle with this; it takes practice, since you will naturally shift your brain to Hindi mode to understand, and may find it easier to stay in Hindi mode while you respond). If you are ever forced to speak in Hindi - in Hindi class, reciting lines for a play for the Hindi school annual program, reading from the prayer book at the temple - make sure you speak with a thick American accent. This is no time to work on your pronunciation. For the greater good - and by that I mean staying single - you must willingly degrade yourself in this area.

RULE #4
NEVER LET THEM SEE YOU COOK

Despite the fact that when your mother grew up in India, she was surrounded by servants and probably never cooked a day in her life, here in America, as a daughter, you are expected to help in the kitchen. As your future husband has yet to be determined, your parents do not know exactly what kind of food you ought to master. Should they teach you Gujarati style vegetables heavy on spice and sugar, or creamy Punjabi dishes? Or would their efforts be better spent teaching you to make Idli and Dosa, so that in-laws from the South will be pleased? Without this knowledge, they will teach you all of it.

On Fridays every couple of months, my family would sit on the family room floor, newspapers laid out in front of us. On the newspaper would lie a stack of baking trays, a few cutting boards, a small dish of water, a box of Gallon-sized freezer bags, and a large metal bowl of dough. My mother would bring over the large pot of potato-and-pea filling that cooked while we ate dinner and sit down as well. We would turn on an Indian movie, my mother would roll out long, thin ovals out of balls of dough, cut them in half, and hand one to each of us. My sister and I would assemble samosas by making cones from the dough, then filling and sealing them before placing them on trays that were filled and frozen. In one sitting, we would make something like five hundred samosas, which could then be thawed and fried whenever we had parties at our house. We did the same thing with other snack foods.

And whenever company was coming over, my sister and I would be summoned to help in the kitchen. My mother said it was to help her because there was so much work to be done. She tried to cover it up by having us polish the silverware, vacuum, dust, and otherwise get the house ready for a party, but inevitably, we would be the ones adding all the ingredients into whatever dishes my mother would be making. Step by step, one person cooked one dish (even if I were adding anything to my dish on the stove, I wasn't to add anything to my sister's; supposedly it would make it too confusing and the ingredients might end up being added twice, but really, I think it was to give us a sense of ownership - and hopefully pride - over the outcome of a particular dish). The only exception was the breads - roti, puri, naan. These were better mass-produced quickly, and so my sister and I would both roll the dough while our mother cooked.

The problem was, while we were doing this out of our innate sense of goodness, this helpfulness always backfired. Even if there were no boys our age coming (and yes, there were times when we wished there were, since some of them were cute), we would have to listen to our mother brag about how we cooked dinner, and point out which dish each person cooked. This was NOT information we wished to go public, but we couldn't exactly refute it, not without coming across as a jerk or embarrassing our mother, neither outcome we desired.

The key to success is not to remember anything that you're being told. Each time you make the same dish, you must force your mother to tell you the ingredients, even if you know them. She must get the sense that you cannot cook except as a kitchen maid, and that is certainly not a trait she will want to brag about. And getting creative in the kitchen is absolutely inexcusable.

Finally, when your mother visits India for a while, and you must cook in her stead, for goodness sake, don't attempt to cook Indian food. Your parents' friends will bring food for you if you really need Indian, and the effort - no matter how disastrous the results - will surely be applauded. Not only that, but this story will be recounted far and wide (by your parents, anyhow; interested mothers-in-law probably wouldn't share this story for fear of generating more competition for their son and, quite possibly, lowering their negotiating status).

RULE #5
CHASE AWAY THE CHAI

This one could perhaps be considered part of the cooking rule, except that with tea, the danger is greater. The evidence is more first-hand, as opposed to anecdotal by your mother, who could very well be exaggerating your cooking prowess. Remember that chai can be served at any time and any place; it is, after all, the national drink of India (if it's not already, it should be!). So always be on your guard. If you arrive at someone's house, and you somehow end up adjacent to the kitchen when tea is being prepared, flee. Visit the bathroom, say you forgot something in the car, do whatever you have to do, but get out. Otherwise, you will be roped into helping in the tea preparation and service.

Why, you may wonder, is it such a bad thing to be helpful when visiting a family friend's home? It isn't, truly it isn't. But tea is an adult drink. Next time you are at a party, take a look during tea time and think about what you see. Adults, relaxing, smiling, chatting with one another, not a child in sight (which is why they are relaxing and smiling). This is when grownups are able to finally take off their parenting shackles and enjoy the company of others like them. The men are free from work, the women have a temporary reprieve from the kitchen (for a few minutes anyhow; soon enough it will be time to take out the appetizers, and then set up the dinner buffet on the kitchen island, and then set out dessert, oh and to make sure there are enough two-liter bottles and styrofoam cups on the counter next to the sink).

They are amongst their peers, and the LAST thing you want to do is to let them see that you belong with them. They need to see you as one of 'the kids' who hang out in the basement (or up in the bedroom of the homeowner's daughter giggling and playing Indian songs). They need to dismiss you as they do the rowdy eight to twelve year old boys who turn on the video game console the minute they arrive and don't stop playing until their parents yell at them that it's time to leave. Stay there, stay hidden as long as you can.

Sometimes, however, you have no choice. The person you are standing closest to volunteers and there's nobody else around and so everyone stops and stares at you, clearly waiting for you to say "of course I'll help," while you curse under your breath at your companion for shoving you into the spotlight. Accept gracefully that you are stuck, and move ahead to plan B.

Come now, you didn't think there was no plan B, did you? What kind of monster do you think

I am, and what kind of survival guide would this really be without a plan B.

Anyhow, there you are, in the kitchen, in the presence of aunties. Most likely it will only be a subset of the entire Aunty collection for the evening, and if you're lucky, the aunties on tea duty are on the younger side (having children too young to be looking at you through a mother-in-law's eyes). But even if this is the case, make sure not to let down your guard, because too much camaraderie with the younger aunties can be fatal. Imagine, if you will, what would happen if, while you merrily chatted with a lower-echelon aunty, another aunty with a marriageable son walks past the kitchen and sees you. Just look at you in there, an absolute vision - feeling comfortable in the kitchen, making chai like a pro, chatting amicably with your peers - you are a domestic diva. From there, it's a short trip to the mental mandap.

But fret not; don't start eyeing all your acquaintances suspiciously figuring out who will be the first to throw you under the lorry. In all likelihood it will either happen accidentally or by someone who wants to make her way onto an Aunty's radar. Just put Plan B into action.

First and foremost, you must understand that Chai is a mysterious and complicated recipe. There is a certain amount of magic passed from generation to generation on the formulation of the perfect combination of this divine concoction. To fully appreciate chai, you must respect and revere the fine history and intricacies that make it the cure of all that ails a true Indian. This is, in fact, how a true Indian would view chai, and knowing and understanding this will empower you.

Step one: insult chai. Don't be too rude, or frankly you risk being shunned from Indian society altogether. They must be only slight insults - perhaps leaning more toward self-effacing than insulting ("I don't see the appeal of a hot drink on a hot day; I'd rather a cola anytime."). Ideally, you come across as silly and childish, and the others think, "she will understand when she gets older."

Step two: the kitchen is a stranger. Sure, you have one in your house, and yes, you've used it from time to time (to make toast and perhaps warm up the odd toaster pastries), but otherwise, you know nothing about its inner workings. Muddle up the most straight-forward task (like boiling water for tea). Over-steep the tea bags. Add too much sugar. Add salt! Confuse the two types of tea (water-based versus milk-based with spices). Whatever you do, make the worst cup of tea you possibly can. Now, you're not trying to poison everyone, just avoid assisting in the future. Be obvious; only do the painfully delinquent moves when the supervising aunty is watching, because you want it known that you cannot make chai without actually ruining other people's evening. Only the kitchen aunty (or aunties) will know, but they will surely tell your mother as they drink tea, and other aunties will overhear. They will, after all, have to explain why it took so long to make tea; they will remake the entire batch before serving, but will let the story live on.

Step three: repeat steps one and two. Once is not enough. If you make a bad enough cup of tea, perhaps you will be lucky enough not to be summoned to help again. Or, more than likely, you will be called more often. Some far-too-kind (or just plain bored) aunty will take you on as her personal project, and vow to teach you how to make tea. Try harder to avoid the kitchen altogether if you see her in the vicinity, as she may volunteer to make tea just to get a chance to work with you again. Think of the glory she would receive if she managed to convert you from a chai-no-sir to a chai-noisseur. Believe me. When faced with that level of determination, you will return for another training session. And perhaps another. You will need to work hard and give her just enough hope for a few lessons (where you still make mistakes, but seem to be trying so hard!), and then go back to being pathetically ignorant. You need to break her; you need for her to decide that she would rather hide from you at tea time than vice versa. Take control of the situation, because to break her, you need to first build up that level of hope, and then send it crashing back to earth.

This may sound a little harsh, but think of the alternative. You let this aunty, who thinks her life is like an Indian movie (let her husband be her hero; let her children live out her dreams; you need not be part of that drama), show off to the world how she changed your life - how she helped you learn to make chai. Next thing you know, your tea-making skills will be in demand wherever you go, whenever Indians are around. And yes, of course, your Marriageability Ranking will be much higher.

RULE #6
MARO THE MIND GAMES

It is by no means an easy task to avoid matrimony as an Indian girl. From the time you hit puberty, your parents are thinking non-stop about how to safely escort you from this vulnerable state into the safety of a good marriage. Truth be told, many parents actually think about this from the moment they learn they're going to have a daughter (be that at birth or during an ultrasound). In their view, their job as parents is not complete until you have been lovingly passed on to another family who will cherish you as much as they have. As long as they have you with them, they must prepare you to be part of another household, to be amongst people who they don't know, and thus whose rules they don't know. They worry that you will not fit in, that you will struggle to adapt, that your new family will not love you as they do. They fear that they will teach you all the wrong things, and that you will find your married life full of strife and hardship.

Undoubtedly, as an Indian girl, you already know this, because you have heard many versions of this Great Sacrifice as a form of discipline. If you have strict parents, this may come across in the form of the Lucky You, which usually starts with the phrase "In my day". As I said before, I never attended any school dances. This was not, by the way, by choice. As my parents explained it, those dances were for American children who don't have other social options. We meanwhile had a large community of Indian families with whom we regularly met. We even had dances, attended only by kids (and a few chaperones, of course) that were, I imagine, just like school dances - with the same cliques of geeks, athletes, rebels, and popular kids as in any other community. The only difference was that these people all had brown skin. We didn't listen to Indian music, or wear Indian clothes, or even eat Indian food - it was catered, but we could go across the street to the sandwich shop if we felt like it).

But here's the thing. Back in my parents' day, there were no such dances. They were not allowed to spend an entire evening with members of the opposite sex unless their parents were around. Their social lives revolved around attending weddings, where you could find four generations of people who had known each other forever. You certainly wouldn't try spending one-on-one time with a boy without half the town knowing about it before the garlands were exchanged.

In other words, we were pretty lucky to even attend these Indian dances. We knew better than to cause any trouble while we were there because if we were growing up in India, we would have had much less freedom. So we would feel like we actually won a battle by being allowed the freedom to attend these Indian dances. I did mention that the parents are pretty wily, didn't I? They got us to see as normal the concept of spending time socially with other Indians, which reinforced the idea that we would need that degree of Indianness in our adult lives in order to be happy.

There are many other instances where the Lucky You technique is used. This example left us all happy, but that isn't always the case. Used sparingly, the Lucky You can be quite effective, so that you barely know it's being used. But overly generous application of the Lucky You can put you instantly in a defensive mode which can only hurt any negotiating attempts. In their day, Indian parents didn't have modern appliances like dishwashers (no, they had cheap labor, and they never did dishes as children); they had to ride a rickshaw to school, not get their own car, so no you cannot go out with your friends. After school, they would have to take the rickshaw directly home and take care of their young cousins or nieces and nephews or do mounds of homework, which was much more plentiful in their day. They did not have as many clothes, or throw them away so nonchalantly; they packed a tiffin with their lunch, and couldn't buy junk from vending machines at school, which didn't exist in their day. It really is impressive how anyone survived in their day, isn't it? You will surely think this, but be aware that talking back, rolling your eyes, or simply walking away will not yield the desired outcome, but rather are likely to lead to escalation.

    Another oft-used technique is the Guilt Trip. This usually is done with a friendly manner, where they seem to be talking to you as adults, and give you the sense that you're actually negotiating for something, but right when you believe you're about to get your way (that you'll be allowed to go to the school dance after all), they abruptly - and unexpectedly - finish with a resigned sigh and a

"Do what you want". If you happen to be in your parents' bedroom, and your mother is lying in her bed, you can clearly picture her flailing her head to the side and putting the back of her hand to her forehead in a melodramatic way. Even if she does not do this, or you are not even in that setting, the image appears, and you know very well just what your insolence is doing to her, and you are forced to ask yourself whether this silly little event is really so important that you would subject your parents to such grief.

Your parents are masters of manipulation. These examples may seem trivial to you right now, but what you may not realize is that in using these techniques throughout your childhood, they are calibrating you to be ideally receptive when it comes time to marry you off. They are honing their skills, finding the perfect balance of these techniques to get the desired outcomes. They are also building up ammunition for future guilt trips. For example, if you try to argue that you never get to do anything, they can remind you that they let you go to those Indian dances you wanted to go to. Pretty devious, isn't it, how they can make you feel guilty about doing something that they want you to do anyhow? Who knows? They may have even suggested the dance to you in the first place.

So how can you win? How can you get what you want without giving them more examples to show how bad a daughter you are? First, you must know yourself. Know what is important to you and whether something is worth fighting for. I used to consider something, rehearse the argument in my head that I would have with my mother, then, knowing how she would react, I would either fix my argument or decide against arguing at all. After all, each time I would lose an argument, I would only strengthen her, and I figured I should save up for something that really mattered to me.

Next, you must be able to recognize the tricks your parents are using, and build an immunity to them. Especially useful is being unaffected by the Guilt Trip, because that is the method parents most often fall back to when trying to marry you off. Just remind yourself that while they are training you, you too are training them. Perhaps you can keep your true feelings to yourself - lull them into a false sense of security by seeming the perfectly compliant daughter throughout your childhood only to blindside them with a strong rebellious streak later in life. Keep your eye on the prize, namely your staying single.

Ultimately, the key to success is being strong. You must find the strength inside yourself to stand up for who you are. Yes, you are Indian, but don't be ashamed of the fact that you are also American (do make sure that you do not, in the process, ever feel ashamed to be Indian; the goal is not to give up your Indianness, just avoid matrimony in the traditional arranged-marriage route unless or until you are ready).

Beware, the stronger you are, the stronger the attacks your parents will launch. You may be seen (only by them, of course) as an 'ungrateful daughter', but don't be blindsided into believing for one minute that your parents actually would move the family back to India. There's two quick reasons why that will never happen. Though they will never admit it, they actually do like living in America. Sure, they miss their families, but the modern conveniences they have here, as well as the alone-time to which they have grown accustomed over the decades, would be too difficult to give up. And yes, when your aunts and uncles come visit from India, they marvel at just how hard your mother's life is, having to do all that work alone without any servants (see, this just proves that 'in their day' life wasn't quite so tough), but inside, your mother knows she wouldn't trade it for anything. She doesn't have to battle with her mother-in-law day after day, or feel like her in-laws are setting her husband against her.

    Your father doesn't have to choose between loyalty to his wife and fealty to his parents. His rank in the family, being the second youngest brother, has been elevated by becoming the foreign son. When he returns to his ancestral home, he is now treated more like a damaad (revered son-in-law - an inherently redundant phrase) than an almost-youngest-son.

And if you don't believe me, pay attention to them on your next trip to India. See how their excitement at returning to their homeland early in the trip turns to exhaustion and an eagerness to return stateside that can only be matched by your own. They may deny it (don't be fool enough to ask), but it's there. Admittedly, it may be harder to sense this change in your father, especially if he's one of those easy-going, happy-go-lucky, fun dads. But then, you wouldn't need to be reading this guide, would you? You wouldn't have any daddy issues you need to resolve, or any inherent prejudice against the institute of marriage. Unless the easy-going nature is coupled with a strong forgetfulness that aggravates not only your mother but even you at times.

But frankly, the psychology of the relationship between your parents is not the central focus of this guide. Sure, it factors into your attempts to remain single. But that is certainly not something you can change, so it is beyond the scope of this guide.

RULE #7
BEWARE THE BIODATA

Sooner or later, your parents are going to declare you 'grown up' and thus ready to be put on the market. First of all, don't mistake this declaration as containing any rights or benefits for you whatsoever, because rather than meaning that they trust you with more freedom, they instead will simply burden you with more responsibility. You will be unfazed by this declaration at first, because you should, honestly, be accustomed to this pattern. At ten, you were declared 'old enough' to mow the lawn (what a great privilege, you thought, until it became a chore done by you and you alone). Your driver's license did not, as you had dreamed, lead to more freedom and time with your school friends. Instead, it meant more trips to the grocery store, and picking up your sister from band practice. During college, you were given your own car at first so that you could commute instead of living in the dorms, and when your course burden grew too great, so that you could drive home every weekend rather than have your parents have to drive out to pick you up Friday afternoon and drop you off Sunday evening. By the way, locking yourself in your bedroom during that time was not the best decision, since you could then not use the excuse that you needed to study for an exam as a reason to stay on campus, since you clearly were given plenty of good, interruption-free study time at home.

"And you wouldn't even have to spend any money or effort having to cook for yourself, because your mother so kindly is cooking your meals for you so that you can just come downstairs for meals," your father would say.

"It would be nice, of course, if you could spend a little time with your sister," they might say. "She does miss you while you're at school all week, you know."

Of course, you and your sister are either talking on the phone almost every day, or, if she happened to have borrowed and ruined your shirt while you were gone, not talking at all. Either way, there's no 'missing you' going on in her world.

But your 'grown up' declaration should be dreaded. It corresponds with your college graduation, or, in their view, the conferring of your MRS degree. If you do not already have a marriage arranged for you at this time, this is when things start to get ugly.

Step one: you must be career-oriented. Pick a college major that allows you to get a job straight out of college, or at least one that shows that you plan to go to medical school. After all, a doctor for a daughter-in-law is still seen as a good thing. The potential in-laws are not so archaic to expect their daughters-in-law to give up their careers, although repeated discussions about how much you love your job will give them pause.

If you pursue a degree that allows you to get a job upon graduation, and you do start to work, then, every time you get sucked into conversation with adults (which, I'm afraid, will happen more often once you're declared 'grown up'), you must discuss how fulfilling work is. Don't brag, but be sure to mention, in response to how they haven't seen you in so long, that you've been working long hours on 'this big project' (even if you decided to bail on a dinner party to stay home and watch an Indian movie with your sister - your parents will never tell because they can't admit that they couldn't convince you to join them, especially if you tell them it's because - as they reminded you - you 'haven't spent time with your sister').

Sidebar - if your parents tell you that you can just 'go there to eat and then go home', don't believe them. If you fall for that logic, well, then you deserve to be there. But you should certainly know that: one - dinner is never served right when you get there, and two - loading up on appetizers and leaving is considered an insult.

If you decide to pursue a career in medicine, well, you're in pretty good shape. You will, of course, be expected to go into Pediatrics or Internal Medicine, or some other field that can later allow you to work part time when you have children. Unless you actually like these fields, I would urge you against it. Emergency medicine, of course, is great for allowing flexible hours, and for working part time, but its reputation for craziness leaves many Aunties and Uncles uneasy, and rightfully so - it would require their son to have a more consistent schedule so that he can always be around to take the kids to school and pick them up in case you're working, and for him to work around your schedule. Traditionally, that is not an arrangement that people wish for their sons (since it makes them seem less the Alpha and more the Beta member of the couple), and so it may work in your favor. Still, as a doctor, you get high ranking on the Marriage Market, but everyone would rather see you marry someone else. And that can work out quite in your favor (but if your parents are hesitant to support your medical aspirations, this is why).

Whatever field of study you choose, do keep in mind that your choice may or may not affect your marriage choice, but it is something that you will live with for the rest of your life, regardless of whether, when, and whom you choose to marry.

That said, you must understand that your parents must remain true to who they are, true to their belief system. And yes, this means that they feel it is their responsibility to create a biodata for you and to find you a suitable husband. Keep in mind that in their day, this was traditional, and this was not challenged, so by not simply going along with their plans, you are pushing them into uncharted territory. I'm not saying you should simply play along and let them marry you off; if you got this message, then I would suggest that you go back and reread from the beginning (starting from the title). I only mean that you will fare better in your pursuits if you understand what you're up against, and yes, in this matter, that includes your parents. Because frankly, if your parents were not pressuring you, you probably wouldn't be reading this.

Accept that somewhere floating out there is or will be a biodata with your name on it. The key is for you to get involved in its creation. Use words that to the untrained eye seem perfectly accurate and desirable, but to anyone that you would even consider marrying would be a warning sign. Parents would love to introduce their son to a woman who is 'homely', and maybe even 'lovely', but the son would be weary of meeting this woman. A 'talented homemaker' would seem straightforward enough, but a boy drawn to someone with that description is going to constantly compare you to his mother. Add more descriptions which will help weed out everyone that you would never want to meet. The beauty of this strategy is that only those who you would never want to marry will respond, which makes the vetting process that much simpler.

RULE #8
SABOTAGE THE SHAADI SHOT

I don't know if this one is even relevant anymore, what with half the planet signed up on Facebook and other social media sites. Nowadays, rather than send out a biodata and marriage photo, your parents could save themselves the effort and simply share your Facebook and LinkedIn profiles.

Let's first understand the process. Your parents create a biodata, and send it out, along with a flattering picture of you, to someone they have learned about from their good friend, or aunt's cousin's daughter's husband, or from a matrimonial ad in an Indian newspaper or on Shaadi.com. The boy's parents receive a stack of these biodata (if they are received by email, the files will be printed at work by the father's secretary, along with the photograph), and the mother and father look through their stack of potential daughters-in-law while enjoying their evening chai and biscuits. Perhaps some Indian music will be playing the background, or else the Indian news on satellite TV. From the kitchen will come the consistent whirring whistle of the pressure cooker. Whatever the case, they will make separate piles for those girls they would like to learn more about and those that should be eliminated altogether. What you need to figure out is how to make your picture stand out just enough so that it gets eliminated right from the start, without even having them read the biodata.

    What makes a bad picture? First, convince your parents that they should send your biodata by email. The quality of a photograph printed on paper will never compare to that of one printed on photo stock. It sends the message that your parents cannot be bothered to pay for a printout of the photograph and for postage. "People these days," the boy's parents will think, "put too much stock in computers. In our day we would write long letters to India. Back then, postage was so expensive we would write to our parents on aerograms, with writing so small and filling every bit of blank space on the page. What, do these people not value the written word? Have they forgotten their heritage?" And boom, you may not even be printed out! Score!

That said, perhaps your parents will share the same viewpoint, and will refuse to resort to something so crass as planning their dear daughter's future on the computer instead of in person (or via a glorified personal resume and mass-copied photograph). How will they pick that picture of you? Well, don't make it easy. At parties, when you do get dressed up in nice Indian clothes, don't stand alone, or you may well be photographed solo. A full-body shot is standard, so always carry something to detract from the picture. When you arrive at a party, scope out the space, and find the best backdrops for photographs. Then avoid them.

Here are a few tips on ways to prevent the marriage picture from being taken. After scoping out the crowd, and making sure there are no potential matches (or parents of matches) present, carry a baby. No parent will send a picture of you carrying a baby. It would put too many questions into the recipient's mind (rather than show you as being nurturing, if you are photographed with the child, people will wonder if that child is yours). That said, the reason you have to make sure there are no potential matches present is because in person, carrying a baby demonstrates that you can be a good mother, and any doubts are easily dispelled through the course of the event. Another thing you should do is always carry a drink (if you are of age, make it alcoholic, otherwise, ask for a frilly umbrella). I am not suggesting that you drink incessantly and make a fool of yourself. Instead, your parents (or whoever they have convinced to photograph you) will not want an image of you presumably drinking alcohol as your marriage photo.

You never want to be caught alone, in front of a gorgeous background. Save the admiring of the scenery for another day, or at least when you're with your friends. Then, when you are photographed, stand in the back, or make sure someone else is behind you. You don't want to make it easy to crop someone else out of the photograph. If you are at a wedding, and happen to be giving a toast, hold the champagne glass in front of you throughout your speech. Of course, pictures of people talking are rarely flattering, so you are probably safe there. But if you take a moment to glance at the happy couple and smile, someone could take a very nice picture of you indeed. So try to give a toast with a group, if you can.

Avoid the photo shoot. If your parents arrange for a photo shoot 'for a nice recent family picture', do not allow yourself to be photographed alone "just to test the lighting." But even if you are naive enough to fall for that, then have fun frustrating your parents. Growl at the camera. Make a funny face. You know the phrase, "make love to the camera"? Try it. Look seductive. But make sure you go overboard with it; be shy now, and your parents have just bought themselves the perfect marriage shot. Open your eyes really wide and smile. Show too much teeth. If you are hesitant to anger or embarrass your parents in public, listen to them. Act like you're trying. Respond to whatever they ask you to do, but just a little too eagerly. That is sure to ruin any photograph. But you must commit to going all out on this one, or they will find something salvageable, and be able to explain away any minor flaws ("oh, poor thing had a cold", or "she was about to sneeze"). You mess this up and you may actually endear yourself to some aunty with that adorable picture.

RULE #9
FLAUNT FACEBOOK:
MAKE YOUR SOCIAL NETWORK YOUR NAUKAR

Regardless of how your marriage photos turn out, any prospective grooms will automatically search for you on Facebook anyhow, so be ready. Taking a non-flattering marriage photo will not get you very far, because if anything in your biodata does appeal to the parents, any boy with any sense will check Facebook to try to find something to rule you out (or, if he is fond of your marriage photo, he will want to see more pictures of you). This is what you want to happen (well, not the 'getting fond of you' part, of course).

Remember that last Indian party you went to? Well, in all likelihood, the whole album is being uploaded right now. Which means that that guy whose parents got your biodata last week is looking at them on his lunch break. So what does your Facebook profile say about you?

Now, you undoubtedly know that if you do have career aspirations, you must make sure that your Facebook profile does not show you drinking, smoking, in any state of dishabille, or standing too closely to someone not your spouse, so it may be somewhat difficult to mess up your Facebook profile for marriage prospects without simultaneously threatening your career prospects. So do keep that in mind.

What can you do? Well, one option is to change your name on your Facebook account so that anyone searching for you cannot find you by your real name. This would be useful if you have many pictures of you that others have posted that you would not want potential employers to find. Of course, you cannot then create a secondary, 'public' account, because anyone that knows you would simply then mark the photos of you with that account, and you're back to square one.

No, coming up with an alter-ego is not the easiest way to go - especially if you are pursuing a career in high-tech where employers would expect that you would have been an early adopter of every social media site, and your absence would be regarded as suspicious. Since any potential in-laws would not think of this, clearly the plan would have the absolute opposite effect of what you want.

Thus we turn to your profile and your posts. If you publicize your religion, now may be a good time to scale back on the godliness. Nothing is so precious to in-laws than a devout daughter-in-law. You may want to convert (at least on Facebook) for the time being. Buddhism is a safe deviation from Hinduism, but perhaps not extreme enough.

Atheism may be declared only by the extremely brave (and most likely, it will be ignored as childish experimentation that you will surely outgrow). Besides, unless you are willing to become an Angry Atheist, posting all sorts of hateful articles about religion and insulting any potential employer in the process, you may want to avoid this approach.

Choosing a Western religion may imply that you are already being brainwashed by 'some boy', because it simply is not within our makeup to be so insolent. You see, as they raise their daughters to be perfectly compliant and accepting of all their teachings, parents see us as being perfectly moldable. They appreciate how easy it is to instill their values into us (at least, those of us who blindly accept their beliefs - or at least give that impression). But that same appreciation melds quickly into fear when the time comes for college (or any independence, for that matter). At that point, any changes in opinion that you may express (you and I would call it 'growth') are attributed to (a.k.a. blamed on) external forces. In their eyes, you would still be the same innocent, compliant, good little Indian girl that you used to be if not for everyone trying to corrupt you. Which, in their eyes, is the goal of everyone in the world: to turn you against your parents. So that Comparative Religions class was so obviously biased against Hinduism, which they just don't understand and simply dismiss because of its polytheistic nature, that they managed to convince you to denounce who you really are. Unless you didn't take a religion class. Then clearly your peers are to blame.

Which brings us back to Facebook. Do you or do you not friend your parents on Facebook? That really depends on your relationship with your parents and your level of comfort with honesty. If you tell your parents everything, then sure. There will be no misunderstandings, no misinterpretations about pictures of you from random parties. If you talk to them about, even before you post on Facebook, that article about sex, drugs, and/or rock and roll, then by all means, friend them. If, on the other hand, you anticipate spending all your visits back home defending your actions, and justifying their continuing to pay tuition, room, board and expenses while you go off and find yourself, then perhaps that isn't the best idea. Just remember, as you use any social media site, that your parents may well still see whatever you post, and you may not be confrontation-free.

RULE #10
MAKE MASALA OF THE
MEET AND GREET

It is entirely possible that you will be so utterly successful in the earlier stages that your parents will simply throw up their hands in despair and give up on you altogether. Nonetheless, I would be remiss if I did not address the Meet and Greet.

Even if your parents have seemingly given up on arranging your marriage, or are otherwise being very supportive of your career aspirations and personal vision for your future, do keep in mind that they are still worried that you will never get married, or if you do, it will be too late for them to get (or to thoroughly enjoy) any grandchildren. If you have heard any comments about how they "aren't as young as they used to be" or "can't do as much as they used to be able to" or begin discussing what they will leave you when they die, realize that they are not simply being responsible adults finally getting around to their estate planning. Oh no, they are taking a more sly approach.

Accepting that you are not to be swayed by their ideas about what is the perfect age to be married - that you should be old enough to have earned your college degree, yet young enough so that when you do have children, you are still overwhelmed enough by the idea of raising a child alone that you will buy a house close to your parents (ideally in the same town) so that you integrate them into your routine and cannot imagine raising your children without them. You will, no doubt, justify this decision to move close to your parents by explaining that it is cheaper than childcare these days, and that you are doing your children a great service by having them grow up knowing their grandparents. This is, of course, true. But if they do their job correctly, you will not realize that it is in fact your parents who came up with this idea, not you.

I am jumping ahead of myself here. This is their ideal vision: that you will marry someone who will not only make you happy and take care of you financially (should you decide to stay home and raise your children), but also sees the wisdom and appeal in living close to your parents. They want you to marry young enough to find someone not quite firmly established in his career that he cannot move to your home town.

And that is why your parents are so eager to find your perfect match. They are hoping to see your children get married, to see not only what a wonderful child they themselves have raised (you), but also how great of parents they were so that you too were able to raise such a wonderful child that is then growing up and getting married so wonderfully. Because what greater compliment is there to a mother than to see her daughter become a wonderful mother? And how can she know how wonderful a mother you have become until your child has reached adulthood? With this ultimate goal in mind, they fear that with your short-sighted desire to stay single, you will stand in the way of their dreams.

But they will never tell you this. At least, not all at once. They will drop tidbits of this information on you subtly, when you least expect it. And you will not get a chance to be annoyed or to do anything about their subtle statements, because the subject will already be changed before you have a chance to even process it.

So I am warning you to know that this is what your parents are thinking about. Always. Even if you manage to prevent them from creating or sending out a biodata and accompanying Marriage Photo, any situation where you may be with them may turn into an unofficial Meet and Greet. You all decide to go out to dinner ("Oh, what a surprise seeing you here. Have you met my daughter?"), or visit the mall ("Oh, what a surprise seeing you here. Have you met my daughter?"), or the not-so-subtle unexpected trips to places that you have never been but somehow came to your parents' minds as a good place to check out ("Oh, what a surprise seeing you here. Have you met my daughter?").

At any time, in any place, you may be surprised with a Meet and Greet. Know that any time you come into contact with a boy your age or his parents, you are in a Meet and Greet. Always be prepared for this, and be ready to put your best foot forward. And by best foot, I mean your best-attempt-to-appear-respectful-while-deflecting-thoughts-of-marriage foot. The key factor to deciding success in these situations is to keep your opponents, I mean the prospective in-laws, off-guard. Don't let them realize that you know full well that this meeting was orchestrated by meddling parents who want to force you into marriage while simultaneously appearing to be casual and supportive. No, you have to play along, but beat them at their game.

Look at the scene from the boy's parents point of view. They are walking through the park/mall/restaurant district, discussing their son's marriage prospects (because that is all that they think about too, after all), when who do they see, but you, a vision of Indian beauty. And what is it that makes you so beautiful (other than your beautiful brown skin, black hair, and Indian curves modestly adorned, of course)? The fact that you are willing to walk in public with your parents. Even with a frown on your face because you're irritated to be dragged out makes you look good because, in the end, you are present. So they approach you and your parents, and they say hello. And how do you greet them? If you say hello, well, look at your fine manners! If, oh my, you put your hands together for a quick "namaste Aunty, namaste Uncle" - based only on force of habit and not because of some deep-seated sense of cultural respect and sensitivity - well, you may as well climb right up on that mental pedestal they've just built for you in their minds. Be sure to catch that look they give each other while you do it. That will tell you how hard you have to work to stop them from calling up the wedding planner that evening. So what can you do to counteract that simple greeting that caught you off-guard, now that they are standing there engaging your family in a casual, and entirely unplanned, conversation?

Phase one - Don't be there. I don't mean physically, because clearly it is too late for that. Mentally, detach yourself from the scene. Either stay on your phone (I know it's dangerous to walk and text, but sometimes you have to make sacrifices for the greater good. Then again, you don't actually have to text; you just have to give the impression that you're mentally unapproachable). Listen to music, jot on a pad of paper, act like you're thinking about something else, whatever.

Phase two - Don't be there physically. If you can manage it convincingly, rush off to say hello to someone you know, even if you don't know that person very well. Or suddenly remember an errand you need to do and rush off to do it. Perhaps a gift for a boss, or something you need to buy for a class, whatever. Or you need to shop ahead of time for something you know is coming up months from now, saying that you're going to be too busy to get it later. Be vague, but don't take too long. Think of something quickly and escape. Of course, you don't want to share all this information; just have it in mind if you're asked a direct question. Because if you stumble over your excuse, you may not be dismissed from the conversation. Go do your shopping (or talking to someone - and in that case, be creative; if you don't actually know the person, tell them you mistook them for someone else and then engage them in some sort of conversation).

You see, there are a few rules that govern the escape, so know them well to use them well. First, you are only allowed one stop. If you are rushing off to buy something, you must go to one store (the one that you happened to see that reminded you of the phantom errand) and return. So pick one with a long line, and from where you can see when the plotters - I mean, parents - have wrapped up their conversation (in which case you can rush out and say you couldn't find what you needed). If you choose a conversation with someone, make sure the person doesn't look rushed; then you'll stand alone and be forced to return quickly.

Second, you must remain focused. Do not get caught in a lie, or you will not be trusted in the future. Do not look only at your short-term desire to avoid a matchmaking session; protect your right to escape in the future. If you head into a store, only to see someone you know, you must brush them off as you keep searching for your shopping item. Storefronts have large windows, through which your mother and the boy's mother are watching you as they compare stories about their children and marvel at how much they have in common.

Finally, don't take too long. You must return before the end of the conversation. Do not let them set up an intimate dinner while you are still in town, especially if you have already shared with your parents the fact that you're looking forward to a long weekend with no plans. To you, that means lying on the couch all weekend watching Indian movies. To them, that means that you have not made any plans with friends, and thus you will be around to help when they invite someone over for dinner that evening.

Phase three - Listen closely but nonchalantly. When you return from your errand, or if you don't escape at all, pay close attention to where the conversation is heading. Your presence may prevent them from being too obvious in their matchmaking efforts, but that just means you have to pay much closer attention to their conversation. Sense when the conversation will lead to an invitation or any plans, and strike preemptively. Mention that you forgot about a huge homework project you have to work on, or a work meeting you forgot about. If your phone beeps when you get an email, send one to yourself to ring so you can interrupt scheming on cue. Or pretend to get an email about some event you forgot about but you're going to go to, okay? Be careful to word the question so that you're not really asking for permission, but rather you're doing it and are simply informing your parents about your plans.

Because that will be noticed. If you, as a grown woman, are asking your parents for permission to have a social life, then you as a daughter-in-law will be just as considerate. You must be respectful and kind, because you don't want to be the kind of person who disrespects her parents in public (or private, for that matter). But you must demonstrate that you have a mind and a life of your own, and that if that patient mask slips slightly from your parents' faces because of irritation, that is acceptable. You are taking advantage of the situation, but not so blatantly that your parents lose face. Because that's not really your goal. You don't want them to be unhappy; you just don't want to be either.

Which brings us to our final rule.

RULE #11
BE YOU, BE TRUE, BINDAAS

You may have found, while reading through this guide, that you don't agree with some of the more underhanded methods suggested to avoid getting roped into marriage. Good. That leads right into my final point. You need to chill, bindaas, relax. I hope that you can see that your parents, as well as the parents of single boys your age, do not wish you ill. They do not wish to force you into an unhappy marriage 'just to get it over with.' All of these adults actually want to get to know you and find two people who are culturally similar and have personalities that will mesh well over a lifetime together. Yes, in their quest to share their wisdom about what does and does not make a successful marriage, these adults may become a little overzealous, to the point of making you feel like a head of cauliflower in a Farmer's Market - up for sale and pointedly scrutinized for any minute flaws.

When the question of marriage is not on the table, these adults are actually very interesting, very kind people who can be at times funny, incredibly helpful, thoughtful beyond belief, and can help you remember what it means to be Indian. Usually, however, the first exposure any girls have to adults is when they reach a marriageable age and are suddenly expected to join their ranks. This can certainly be disconcerting, and with good reason. It is thus easy to simply rebel against the whole concept of marriage - arranged or otherwise - until such time as you suddenly feel like it's too late and that you're never going to find anyone.

Here's the thing. It will happen, and you will be happy. Or rather, when you remember, as you have known all along, that you don't need someone else to make you happy, you will find your perfect match. Until then, you risk jumping into marriage only out of fear of being alone, and then your path to happiness will be that much more arduous.

Instead, never forget who you are, and what you believe in. Never forget that your parents love you and wish you the best. Push your limits - by all means, do so as much as you feel comfortable doing - but not to the point that when you do get married and have children, they have been so irreparably hurt by you that they will not wish to have a relationship with their grandchildren. Oh, who am I kidding? Their relationship with their grandchildren will be fine; the only question is whether they'd let you in the house with them.

Finally, make sure not to be so focused on avoiding that Evil Institution of Marriage that you don't open your heart enough to that perfect someone if he happens to show up in all the wrong ways at exactly the wrong time (such as, hypothetically, if you happen to agree to meet some guy that your parents forced you to meet as a peace offering before you leave town for graduate school, and he ends up being perfect for you, except that you're not planning to get married for at least three years, but then he ends up moving to the same town as you a year later, and you're both still single. And suppose hypothetically that he keeps asking you out, and you finally agree, counting on finding that flaw - because why else would he agree to let his parents set him up (ignoring the fact that you, too, let your parents set you up), but instead you find a sweet, funny, intelligent, and attractive man whose company you thoroughly enjoy, and when you finally do graduate, in lieu of a graduation party, you plan a wedding and live happily ever after).

    I'm not saying this hypothetical situation has ever arisen or would ever arise, but you certainly don't want to miss out on meeting some interesting people because you are too focused on avoiding matrimony. Even if you don't end up marrying any of the men to whom you are introduced, it never hurts to make a friend. Unless that friend is a wannabe cage fighter who likes to take you on dates to a training ring to spar. Then you may want to limit your encounters to Facebook. Otherwise, you never know whose brother, or roommate, or cousin, or best friend may still be single and perfect for you when you are ready to circle the blessed flame.

ABOUT THE AUTHOR

Nivi R. Engineer has never had a biodata with her name on it. Of course, she never gave her parents a chance, beating her siblings to the mandap by thirteen years. She holds an English degree, focusing on Creative Writing, from Case Western Reserve University, and a Master's Degree in Computer Science from Washington University in St. Louis. She now lives in Cleveland, Ohio with her husband, three kids, and puppy.

Made in the USA
Lexington, KY
24 September 2012